The Birds of Killingworth

Based on a poem by Henry Wadsworth Longfellow

Robert D. San Souci

pictures by Kimberly Bulcken Root

Dial Books for Young Readers

New York

For Pat Kite,
my friend and fellow writer
who shares a love of the natural world
R.D.S.S.

For Janna
K.B.R.

Published by Dial Books for Young Readers
A division of Penguin Putnam Inc.
345 Hudson Street
New York, New York 10014
Text copyright © 2002 by Robert D. San Souci
Pictures copyright © 2002 by Kimberly Bulcken Root
All rights reserved
Designed by Lily Malcom
Text set in Centaur
Printed in Hong Kong on acid-free paper
1 3 5 7 9 10 8 6 4 2

Library of Congress Cataloging-in-Publication Data
San Souci, Robert D.
The birds of Killingworth: based on a poem by Henry Wadsworth Longfellow/
by Robert D. San Souci; pictures by Kimberly Bulcken Root.—1st ed.
p.   cm.
Summary: When her father persuades their colony to kill all the birds because
they are eating the crops, Almira joins the schoolmaster in proving that the
birds are not only beautiful, but, like all creatures, serve a larger purpose.
ISBN 0-8037-2111-0 (hc.)
[1. Birds—Fiction. 2. Ecology—Fiction.] I. Longfellow, Henry Wadsworth,
1807–1882. Birds of Killingworth. II. Root, Kimberly Bulcken, ill. III. Title.
PZ7.S1947Bi   2002
[E]—dc21   99-42657   CIP

The illustrations were created on Arches 140-pound hot-press
watercolor paper with watercolor and pencil.

Almira Case paused as she swept the kitchen to listen to the songs of birds through an open window. From the garden of the tidy farmhouse, from the eaves of the barn and sheds, from the fields and orchards came waves of joyous melody.

"Isn't their music lovely?" she asked her father, who sat eating his breakfast.

"I don't call that squawking 'music,'" grumbled Squire Case. He leaned out the window and shook his fist at a crow perched saucily on the fence. "Thief! You eat my corn as fast as it ripens. But I'll soon end your robbery!"

"What do you mean, Father?" Almira asked.

"I have called the farmers and townsfolk to a meeting this very day," he answered. "I have a plan to rid us of the birds that destroy our crops."

"But, Father," Almira cried, "the world would be poorer without their songs!"

"Tut!" Squire Case exclaimed. "Without birds there will be more corn and wheat and rye to sell. When we prosper, so does the whole of Connecticut colony. So no more protests, Daughter!"

Almira was silent. But secretly she decided to attend the meeting and see what her father's plan was all about.

Promptly at noon Squire Case set out for the meeting hall. In his grandest wig and finest coat he looked every inch the richest farmer in Connecticut. When he passed beneath trees filled with songbirds, he angrily swung his walking stick to lop off the heads of lilies.

Behind him Almira knelt to gather the flowers in her apron, planning to place them on her mother's grave later. Suddenly the schoolmaster, Noah Arden, stumbled into her.

"Excuse me, Mistress Case," the flustered young man said, helping her up.

"Thank you, Master Arden," Almira said, her heart beating faster.

"Are you going to the meeting?" he asked, blushing. "If so, may I walk you there?"

"Yes!" she answered. "I am worried that my father may intend to harm the poor birds."

"So am I," said Noah as they hurried on together.

The meeting hall was filled with farmers, field hands, millers, merchants, bakers, barrel makers, goodwives—all whose living depended on the crops of local fields and orchards.

"The time has come to put an end to the birds and the ruin they bring us," Squire Case declared. "I propose that we pay any hunter who kills a full-grown bird. Without parents to tend them, the young in their nests will also perish."

The townsfolk clapped and cried, "Yes! Yes!"

Almira jumped to her feet, forgetting her desire for secrecy. "The birds give us their sweet songs every day. Would you kill them to gain a few grains of corn or a stray cherry?"

"Yes, miss!" her father thundered. "Each grain of corn or cherry stolen is a penny taken from our pockets! You would ruin us for a bird's twittering."

The crowd began to laugh, but they quieted as Noah rose to speak. "How can I teach your children to show mercy to the weak if you contradict my lessons?" he asked. "And surely the birds have some part in heaven's plan. Who are we to challenge the balance of creation?"

"Who are *we*, Schoolmaster?" Squire Case asked. "*We* are the ones who pay your wages. What is best for the town is best for you."

Noah sat down like a scolded child, leaving Almira standing by herself as Squire Case announced that the meeting was ended.

When Noah asked to walk Almira to the churchyard, she said, "I would rather go alone." So they went their separate ways.

Hunters from far and wide came to Killingworth to shoot or trap birds and collect their payment. The songs of finches and meadowlarks were stilled, as were the loud caws of ravens and the soft coos of mourning doves. Innocent bluebirds, hawks, and owls perished along with their guiltier cousins—the crows, blue jays, and blackbirds that sometimes raided farmers' fields or orchards. With their parents slain, the newly hatched young were left to die of hunger.

Heavyhearted, Almira went about her chores. Her father, angry that she had challenged him in public, spoke to her only to report how many more birds had been killed.

One afternoon Almira listened in
distress as tiny robins in a nearby tree
called for parents the hunters had killed.
Unable to ignore their misery, she climbed
the tree and gently lifted down the nest.
Holding it in her apron, she ran as
fast as she could to the schoolhouse.
When she burst into the schoolroom,
Noah cried, "Mistress Case!"

Almira took Noah aside. "You are the only other
person concerned about the birds," she said. "Help me
rescue their young and tend them till they are grown."

"If your father finds out," Noah said, "I will lose
my living."

"I feared that might be your answer," said Almira sadly.

"Yet, no matter the cost, I will help," the schoolmaster declared.
"I believe the birds have a part in heaven's purpose. And," he added,
"I am ashamed that I left you to stand alone before your father and
the town."

"That is past," Almira said, touching his arm. "Together we may
be able to undo some of their harm."

"My pupils will help us," Noah said. "They are filled with grief
over what has happened."

Secretly Almira, Noah, and the children began to gather
helpless newborn birds from trees and hedgerows and the
eaves of barns.

The rescuers brought the tiny birds to the schoolhouse and placed them in hastily built cages. They fed the cagelings with insects and worms, which were plentiful in Killingworth because there were no adult birds to eat them.

As spring turned to summer, the air was filled with the ever-louder chirring and whirring, buzzing and humming, clicking and ticking of insects. Locusts and grasshoppers laid waste to farms and fields, eating every ear of corn and grain of wheat, every leaf and stalk. Worms swarmed orchards and bored into apples and peaches. In the townsfolks' gardens, slugs and snails dined upon lettuce and parsley.

Goodwives and shopkeepers alike found their cupboards and pantries, cellars and storerooms invaded by beetles and weevils, spiders and flies. In town the insects spread into jam pots, milk pitchers, flour bins, and molasses jars. In the country they overran hayricks, corncribs, apple barrels, and granaries.

Each tree was strung with caterpillars that dropped pell-mell on passersby. Every walk was spoiled by the pests that fell on bonnet and hat, jacket and shawl like fat, curling raindrops. Soon no woman went out of doors without a parasol, and men walked under open umbrellas.

"Tut!" cried Squire Case when he found beetles in his wig, moths in his coat, and a family of crickets in his finest shoes. "Tut! Tut!" he exclaimed as he and his workers fought to save the cornstalks and cherry trees from the insect invaders. "Tut! Tut! Tut!" he moaned when he saw that the harvest would be the poorest ever.

After that hot, never-to-be-forgotten summer came a dry, dismal autumn. A few brown leaves clung to trees that had once burned flame-bright each fall. The wind moaned through bare branches, mourning the death of the birds and the dying land.

But in the schoolhouse, lessons began again to the birds' songs. Though food and fuel were scarce that winter, the rescuers dutifully tended the birds. When snow shrouded the fields and woods, Almira felt her heart warm as she worked beside Noah Arden.

On the first morning of the following spring, Almira found her father staring miserably out the parlor window. From beyond came only the cheerless drone of insects.

"Father, what is wrong?" she asked.

"My heart breaks when I look at the barren land," he answered. "I have brought us all to the edge of ruin. Daughter, I confess that I was wrong and you were right. The harm done by a few birds is a small price to pay for the good that all of them do. I wish I could recall the birds."

Almira gave a happy cry and clasped her hands. "Promise never to harm them again," she said, "and you shall have your wish."

"I give my word," said her father. "But how is it possible?"

"You will see," said Almira. "Just gather the townsfolk in the square." And she hurried toward the schoolhouse.

So it was that the people of the town were treated to a strange and wonderful sight. Almira and Noah led a parade of schoolchildren with cages toward the town square. Songs of countless birds filled the air with lovely melodies.

"Father," cried Almira, "set the first ones free!"

Squire Case eagerly unlatched the nearest cage, and four robins soared into the air. Quickly all the cages were thrown open, and the birds flocked to the nearby fields and woods in search of nesting places. They feasted on the hordes of beetles, snails, and other pests; soon the countryside was alive with their wild, sweet music.

They sang still louder on the day of Almira and Noah's wedding. Choir upon choir serenaded the new bride and groom. And as the couple strolled hand in hand, the birds' songs rose in waves of joyous caroling that brought heaven near to the sunny farms of Killingworth.

Author's Note

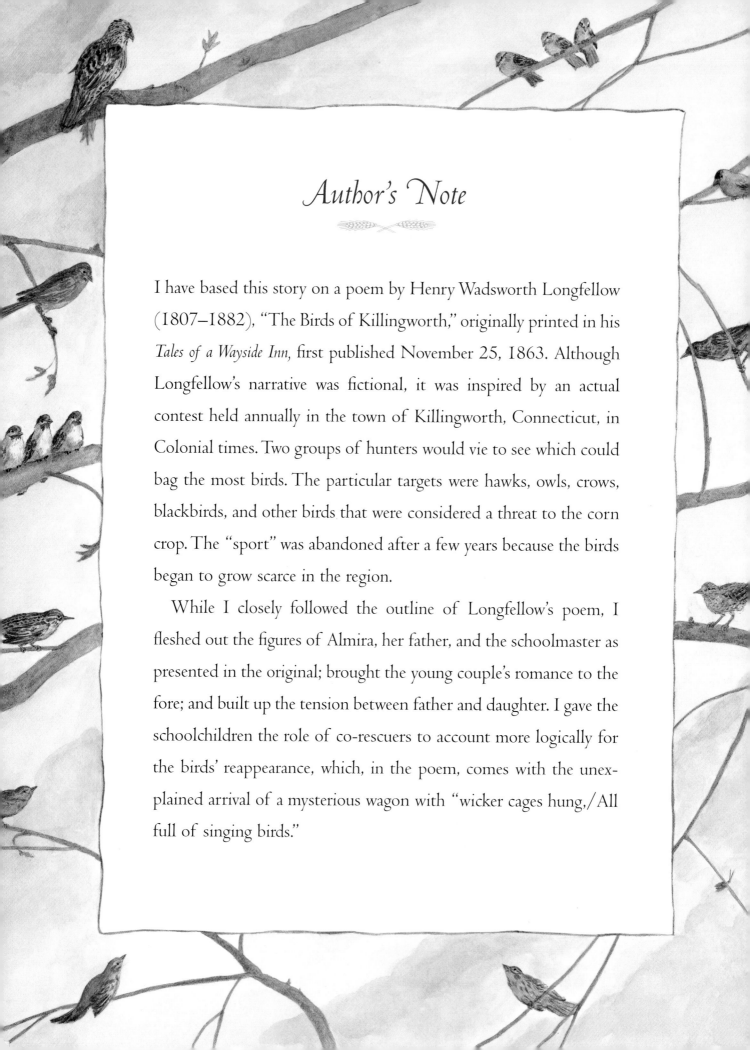

I have based this story on a poem by Henry Wadsworth Longfellow (1807–1882), "The Birds of Killingworth," originally printed in his *Tales of a Wayside Inn*, first published November 25, 1863. Although Longfellow's narrative was fictional, it was inspired by an actual contest held annually in the town of Killingworth, Connecticut, in Colonial times. Two groups of hunters would vie to see which could bag the most birds. The particular targets were hawks, owls, crows, blackbirds, and other birds that were considered a threat to the corn crop. The "sport" was abandoned after a few years because the birds began to grow scarce in the region.

While I closely followed the outline of Longfellow's poem, I fleshed out the figures of Almira, her father, and the schoolmaster as presented in the original; brought the young couple's romance to the fore; and built up the tension between father and daughter. I gave the schoolchildren the role of co-rescuers to account more logically for the birds' reappearance, which, in the poem, comes with the unexplained arrival of a mysterious wagon with "wicker cages hung,/All full of singing birds."